P9-CSF-436

ADAM, ADAM, What Do You See?

This book belongs to

Trinity Lutheran Church

Donated By: The Christiansen's
Monique, Dave, Marc
Jenna & Deven

In honor of Christmas 2001
In the year of the Sept 11th 2001
Tragedy in NY City.

To Bobby Tollison, our friend and pastor.
—bmj and ms

Published in Nashville, Tennessee, by Tommy Nelson®, a division of
Thomas Nelson, Inc.

Library of Congress Cataloging-in-Publication Data

Martin, Bill, 1916–
    Adam, Adam, what do you see? / written by Bill Martin, Jr and Michael Sampson ;
  illustrated by Cathie Felstead.
        p. cm.
    Summary: Presents, in rhymed and illustrated text, a variety of questions and answers
  about Biblical characters and events from the Old and New Testaments.
    ISBN 0-8499-7614-6
      1. Bible—Miscellanea—Juvenile literature. 2. Bible—Quotations—Juvenile literature [1.
  Bible—Miscellanea. 2. Questions and answers. 3. Christian life] I. Sampson, Michael R.
  II. Felstead, Cathie. III. Title.

  BS612 .M37 2000
  220.9'505--dc21

                                                          00-036126

Printed in the United States of America
00 01 02 03 04 PHX 9 8 7 6 5 4 3 2 1

Bill Martin Jr and Michael Sampson

ADAM, ADAM, what Do You See?

illustrated by

Cathie Felstead

Tommy
NELSON®

Thomas Nelson, Inc.
Nashville

**Adam, Adam,
What do you see?**

I see creation all around me.

Genesis 2:4–25

Noah, Noah,
What do you see?

I see animals in the ark with me.

Genesis 7:1–8:22

Abraham, Abraham,
What do you see?

I see a starry sky blinking at me.
Genesis 22:15–18

Joseph, Joseph,
What do you see?

I see father with a coat for me.

Genesis 37:3–4

Moses, Moses,
What do you see?

I see the Red Sea parting for me.

Exodus 14:15–31

Samson, Samson,
What do you see?

I see the strength God gave me.
Judges 14:5–6

**Ruth, Ruth,
What do you see?**

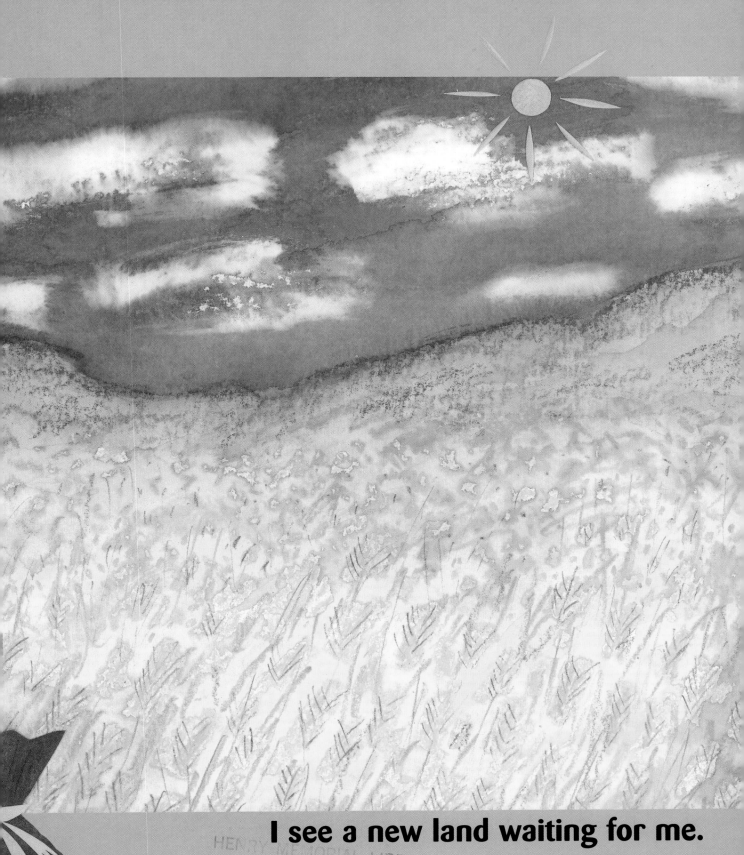

I see a new land waiting for me.

Ruth 1:16–22

David, David,
What do you see?

Esther, Esther, What do you see?

I see the king listening to me.

Esther 5:1–8, 7:3–4

Mary, Mary,
What do you see?

I see Baby Jesus looking at me.

Luke 2:6–7

John, John,
What do you see?

I see God's Son baptized by me.

Matthew 3:13–17

Peter, Peter,
What do you see?

I see miracles all around me.

Luke 5:4–7

**Paul, Paul,
What do you see?**

I see an earthquake setting me free.

Acts 16:25–26

Little Child, Little Child,
What do you see?

I see Jesus watching over me.
Matthew 19:13–14

Jesus, Jesus,
What do you see?

I see Adam, Noah, Abraham, Joseph, Moses, Samson, Ruth, David, Esther, Mary, John, Peter, Paul, and a little child—all seeking me. **THAT'S WHAT I SEE!**

Proverbs 8:17